NO LONGER PROPERTY
SEATTLE PUBL...

D0119105

RECEIVED

JUL 09 20...

Douglass-Truth Branch Library

The Magic of We

Written by Danielle Anderson-Craig

Illustrations by Carly Dooling

THIRD MAN BOOKS

NASHVILLE, TENNESSEE

For music and more information:
http://thirdmanbooks.com/themagicofwe
password: marshmallowmast

"I Know What I Look Like to You"
Written by Ikey Owens - Eugenspusher (ASCAP)

Recorded at: Mass Crush, Austin, Texas
Recording Engineer: Alec Esh
Edit and Mix by: Alec Esh at Mass Crush
Executive Producers: Ikey Owens & Alec Esh
Produced by: Ikey Owens
Recording Engineer: Alec Esh
Mixing Engineer: Alec Esh
Rhodes, Korg Polysix, & Juno-106 performed by: Ikey Owens
Eps-16+ drum programming written by: Alec Esh

"Promise That You Will" is an interpretation of "Sing About Me, I'm Dying of Thirst"
(Bergman/Bergman/Jones/Lamar)
Hard Working Black Folks Inc / Top Dawg Music / W B Music Corp (ASCAP)

Ikey Owens - Keyboards
Dominic John Davis - Bass
Poni Silver - Drums
Tracked at the Casino Studio by Eric Masse in Nashville, Tennessee
Executive Producer: Ikey Owens and Michael Lee

The Magic of We. Copyright © 2018 by Danielle Anderson-Craig. All rights reserved. No part of this book may be used or reproduced in any manner whatsoever without written permission except in the case of brief quotations embedded in critical articles and reviews. For information: Third Man Books, LLC, 623 7th Ave S, Nashville, Tennessee 37203.

Printed in New Brighton, Minnesota.

Library of Congress Cataloging-in-Publication Data

Names: Craig, Danielle Anderson, author. I Dooling, Carly, illustrator.
Title: The magic of we / written by Danielle Anderson-Craig ; illustrations
  by Carly Dooling.
Description: First edition. I Nashville, Tennessee : Third Man Books, (2017)
  I Summary: A rhythmic celebration of love and friendship comparing time
  together to such magical experiences as seeing a collection of castles
  beneath the sea.
Identifiers: LCCN 2017008404 I ISBN 9780991336142 (hardcover)
Subjects: I CYAC: Love- -Fiction. I Friendship- -Fiction. I Imagination- -Fiction.
Classification: LCC PZ7.1.C7 Mag 2018 I DDC (E)- -dc23
LC record available at https://lccn.loc.gov/2017008404

FIRST EDITION
Illustrations by Carly Dooling.
Cover and layout design by Jessica Yohn.

The Magic of We

Being with you...

is like closing my eyes with my head toward the sky;

warm, vast, and orange, too.

Being with you...

is like riding a horse the size of hillsides,

my hair whipped into the rhythm of its mane;

wild, free,

and safe, too.

Being with you is a collection of castles beneath the sea;

breathtaking, majestic, and surprising, too.

Being with you is sailing a chocolate lake

in a graham cracker boat with a marshmallow mast.

I have everything I need.

Being with you is like holding a mirror to another mirror;

infinite, interesting,

enormous and small all at once.

Being with you is taking a nap at the bottom of the sea under a blanket

of starfish, with gills to breathe easy, merfolk singing me to sleep,

an army of sea dragons keeping my dreams sweet;

cozy, calm, and quiet, too.

Being with you is eating breakfast in my favorite pajamas with all seventeen of my stuffies.

I am right where I belong.

Being with you

is my favorite thing to do,

whether we rest

or we roam.

Being with you

is the best being I do,

because being with you